Before They Were President

BEFORE RONALD REAGAN WAS PRESIDENT

Gareth Stevens PUBLISHING

By Therese M. Shea

Please visit our website, www.garethstevens.com. For a free color catalog of all our high-quality books, call toll free 1-800-542-2595 or fax 1-877-542-2596.

Cataloging-in-Publication Data

Names: Shea, Therese M.
Title: Before Ronald Reagan was president / Therese M. Shea.
Description: New York : Gareth Stevens Publishing, 2019. | Series: Before they were president | Includes glossary and index.
Identifiers: ISBN 9781538232521 (pbk.) | ISBN 9781538229118 (library bound) | ISBN 9781538232538 (6pack)
Subjects: LCSH: Reagan, Ronald–Juvenile literature. | Reagan, Ronald–Childhood and youth–Juvenile literature. | Presidents–United States–Biography–Juvenile literature.
Classification: LCC E877.S45 2019 | DDC 973.92'7092 B–dc23

First Edition

Published in 2019 by
Gareth Stevens Publishing
111 East 14th Street, Suite 349
New York, NY 10003

Designer: Laura Bowen
Editor: Therese Shea

Photo credits: Cover, p. 1 (Reagan portrait) Harpsichord246/Wikimedia Commons; cover, p. 1 (background) Silver Screen Collection/Moviepix/Getty Images; cover, pp. 1–21 (frame) Samran wonglakorn/Shutterstock.com; p. 5 AFP/Stringer/Getty Images; p. 7 (inset) Courtesy Ronald Reagan Library/MartinHagberg-commonswiki/Wikimedia Commons; p. 7 (main) Michael Rougier/The LIFE Images Collection/Getty Images; pp. 9, 11, 15 Bettmann/Getty Images; p. 13 Hulton Archive/Getty Images; p. 17 Courtesy of the Ronald Reagan Presidential Library/Happyme22/Wikimedia Commons; p. 19 Bill Ray/The LIFE Picture Collection/Getty Images; p. 21 (bottom) Hohum/Wikimedia Commons, p. 21 (top) MartinHagberg-commonswiki/Wikimedia Commons.

Printed in the United States of America

CPSIA compliance information: Batch #CW19GS: For further information contact Gareth Stevens, New York, New York at 1-800-542-2595.

CONTENTS

Words in the glossary appear in **bold** type the first time they are used in the text.

A MAN OF MANY CAREERS

Most young people dream about what they'll be when they're older. Many say they want to be an actor. Some would love to be an **athlete**. Still others want to be the president of the United States. Ronald Reagan was all these things—and more!

Reagan had many careers, or jobs, even before he became the 40th president of the United States. He's remembered for being a great speaker and for leading the United States toward the end of the **Cold War**.

Presidential Preview

So far, Reagan is the only movie actor to become US president. However, he had a career in **politics** for some years before his presidency.

REAGAN WAS KNOWN AS "THE GREAT COMMUNICATOR" BECAUSE OF HIS EXCELLENT SPEAKING SKILLS. HERE, HE SPEAKS IN FRONT OF THE BERLIN WALL IN GERMANY, WHICH WAS TORN DOWN NEAR THE END OF THE COLD WAR.

ILLINOIS BOY

Ronald Wilson Reagan was born in Tampico, Illinois, on February 6, 1911. His father was John Edward "Jack" Reagan, and his mother was Nelle Wilson Reagan. Ronald had an older brother named Neil.

During Ronald's childhood, his family moved around a lot. In 1920, they settled in Dixon, Illinois. His father opened a shoe store there.

As a teen, Ronald was good at sports and acted in school plays. He was the student body president of Dixon High School. During summer vacations, he worked as a **lifeguard**.

Presidential Preview

Ronald's father called him "Dutch." This name would stick with him throughout his life.

NEIL AND RONALD

RONALD WAS 1 YEAR OLD IN THIS PHOTO. HIS OLDER BROTHER NEIL IS ON THE LEFT.

RONALD'S HIGH SCHOOL FOOTBALL TEAM

COLLEGE AND RADIO

Ronald Reagan began studying at Eureka College in Illinois in 1928. He ran track, played football, and was captain of the swim team. He also acted in school plays and was class president during his senior year.

After leaving college in 1932, Reagan became a radio sports announcer in Iowa. He called himself "Dutch Reagan." He was well known across the state for announcing the Chicago Cubs baseball games. But Reagan wasn't at the games. He reported the games using printed messages from a **teletype** machine!

Presidential Preview

Reagan studied **economics** and **sociology** at Eureka College.

Reagan earned $5 for his first radio job, announcing a game for the University of Iowa football team.

INTO ACTING

Reagan went to the Chicago Cubs spring training camp in California in 1937. While he was there, he decided to try to become an actor. He got a contract with Warner Brothers and began his movie career. He made over 50 movies!

During World War II (1939–1945), Reagan served in the army in Los Angeles, California, making movies that trained soldiers. From 1947 to 1952, Reagan was president of the Screen Actors Guild. He worked to keep **communists** out of this group.

Presidential Preview

While Reagan was US president, he continued to fight against communism and communist countries, especially the Soviet Union.

Reagan played George Gipp in a 1940 movie called *Knute Rockne—All American.* "The Gipper" was another name he was called later in life.

LIFE CHANGES

In 1949, Ronald Reagan met an actress named Nancy Davis. They married in 1952 and had two children, Patricia and Ronald.

Reagan acted less in the 1950s. He became a host for a TV show called *General Electric Theatre*. He also traveled to General Electric factories and gave speeches supporting the company. He said he learned a lot about speaking to people during this time. Because he was afraid of flying, he traveled by train. He spent a lot of time reading and thinking about politics.

Presidential Preview

Ronald Reagan married actress Jane Wyman in 1940. They had two children, Maureen and Michael, but they divorced, or ended their marriage, in 1948. Reagan was the first divorced president.

NANCY REAGAN BECAME ONE OF RONALD'S MOST TRUSTED ADVISORS WHEN HE BECAME PRESIDENT.

SHIFTING VIEWS

Growing up, Ronald Reagan had been a Democrat. In the 1950s, however, his views began to change. He thought the US government was becoming too large and was spending too much money. Reagan officially became a Republican in 1962.

In 1964, Reagan worked on the **campaign** for Republican presidential **candidate** Barry Goldwater. He gave a speech on TV supporting Goldwater called "A Time for Choosing." The speech made Reagan a star of the Republican Party.

Presidential Preview

"A Time for Choosing" is thought to be one of the most successful political speeches ever.

Reagan's speech supporting Barry Goldwater raised over $1 million for Goldwater's campaign. However, Goldwater lost the election to Lyndon B. Johnson.

REAGAN AND GOLDWATER

HIS FIRST ELECTION

In 1966, Ronald Reagan announced that he was running for governor of California. Democratic governor Pat Brown was hoping to be reelected. Brown tried to use Reagan's movie career against him and claimed Reagan didn't have the knowledge to serve as governor.

However, many people liked Reagan's ideas about state government as well as his sense of humor. He seemed less like a movie star and more like an ordinary person who wanted to improve the state. Reagan won the election by almost 1 million votes!

Presidential Preview

Ronald Reagan tried to become the Republican candidate for US president in 1968, but Richard Nixon was chosen instead.

Ronald Reagan and Nancy Reagan celebrate his 1966 election win in Los Angeles, California.

GOVERNOR REAGAN

As governor of California, Reagan put some of his ideas into action. By raising taxes, he erased the state's budget deficit, which occurs when a government spends more money than it brings in.

Reagan served two terms as governor of California. He chose not to seek reelection for a third term. In 1976, Reagan campaigned to be the Republican Party's presidential candidate. However, Gerald Ford, who was president at the time, was chosen instead. Reagan was ready to try again in 1980.

Presidential Preview

At the 1976 Republican National **Convention**, people were divided about whether they wanted Gerald Ford or Ronald Reagan as the Republican presidential candidate. It was a close vote, but Ford won.

Reagan's past as a Hollywood actor stayed with him throughout his political career. He sometimes repeated lines from movies or even dressed as a cowboy, as he did in some of his films.

THE 40TH PRESIDENT

In 1980, Ronald Reagan was finally chosen as the Republican candidate for the presidential election. Democrat Jimmy Carter was running for reelection. In Reagan's campaign, he famously asked voters, "Are you better off now than you were 4 years ago?" At the time, the economy was struggling, and Americans were being held **hostage** in Iran. Many Americans thought a new leader was needed to address these problems.

Ronald Reagan easily won the election and became the 40th US president. He would go on to be reelected in 1984.

Presidential Preview

On March 30, 1981, a man named John Hinckley Jr. shot Ronald Reagan in Washington, DC. Reagan survived and returned to work a few weeks later.

Reagan's Road to the Presidency

1911 Ronald Wilson Reagan is born on February 6 in Tampico, Illinois.

1928 He begins studying at Eureka College.

1932 He becomes a radio sports announcer in Iowa.

1937 He begins his acting career in Hollywood.

1947 He is elected president of the Screen Actors Guild.

1952 He marries actress Nancy Davis.

1962 He officially becomes a Republican.

1964 He gives a speech called "A Time for Choosing."

1966 He wins the election for governor of California.

1968 He runs for president, but Richard Nixon is chosen as the Republican candidate.

1976 He runs for president, but Gerald Ford is chosen as the Republican candidate.

1980 Ronald Reagan is elected the US president.

REAGAN SWORN INTO OFFICE, 1981

PRESIDENT REAGAN

GLOSSARY

athlete: someone who is physically fit and takes part in sporting events

campaign: a series of activities to reach a goal, such as to win an election

candidate: a person who is trying to be elected

Cold War: the nonviolent conflict between the United States and the Union of Soviet Socialist Republics (USSR) during the second half of the 20th century

communicator: one who shares thoughts or feelings by sound, movement, or writing

communist: a person who believes in communism, or a way of organizing society in which the government owns the things that are used to make and transport products and there is no privately owned property

convention: a large meeting of people who come to a place for usually several days to talk about work or other interests or to make decisions as a group

economics: the science having to do with the process or system by which goods and services are produced, sold, and bought

hostage: someone who is being held against their will

lifeguard: a person whose job is to protect swimmers from drowning

politics: the activities of the government and government officials

sociology: the study of society, social institutions, and social relationships

teletype: a printing tool somewhat like a typewriter used to send and receive messages

FOR MORE INFORMATION

Books

Britton, Tamara L. *Ronald Reagan.* Minneapolis, MN: Big Buddy Books, 2017.

Duffield, Katy S. *Ronald Reagan.* Mankato, MN: Childs World, 2016.

Tucker, Rosalyn. *Ronald Reagan.* North Mankato, MN: Capstone Press, 2014.

Websites

Biography: President Ronald Reagan
www.ducksters.com/biography/uspresidents/ronaldreagan.php
Read what happened during Reagan's presidency.

Ronald Reagan
www.whitehouse.gov/about-the-white-house/presidents/ronald-reagan/
Check out the official White House report of Reagan's life.

Ronald Reagan: A Time for Choosing
www.americanrhetoric.com/speeches/ronaldreaganatimeforchoosing.htm
Watch the speech that launched Reagan's political career.

Publisher's note to educators and parents: Our editors have carefully reviewed these websites to ensure that they are suitable for students. Many websites change frequently, however, and we cannot guarantee that a site's future contents will continue to meet our high standards of quality and educational value. Be advised that students should be closely supervised whenever they access the internet.

INDEX

Before They Were President

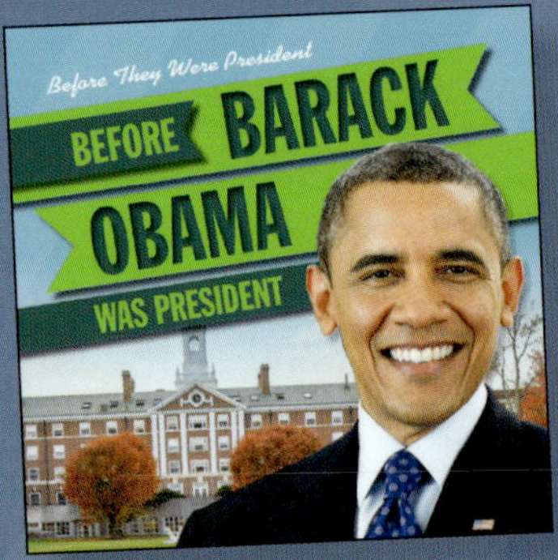

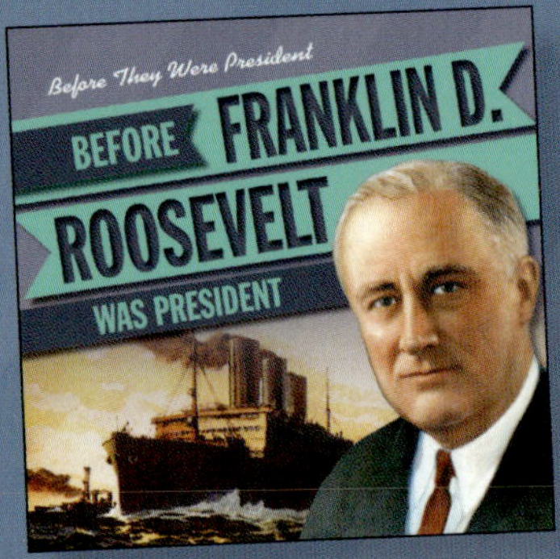

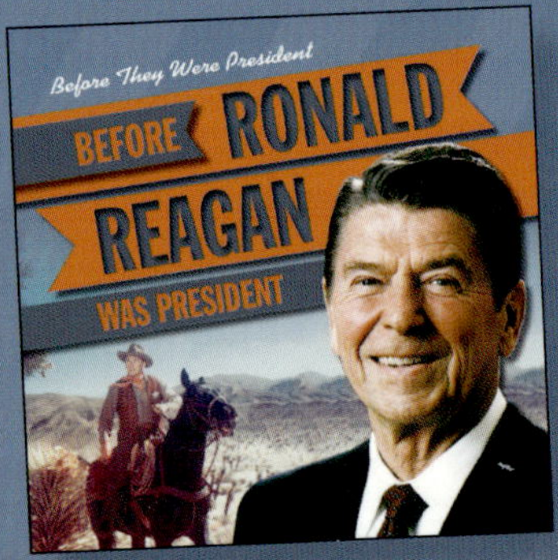

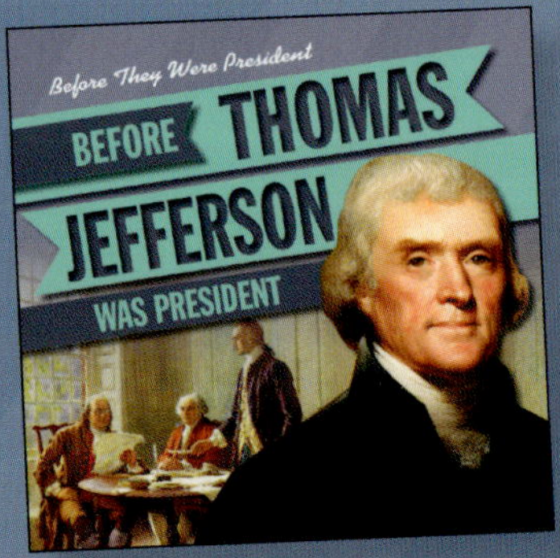

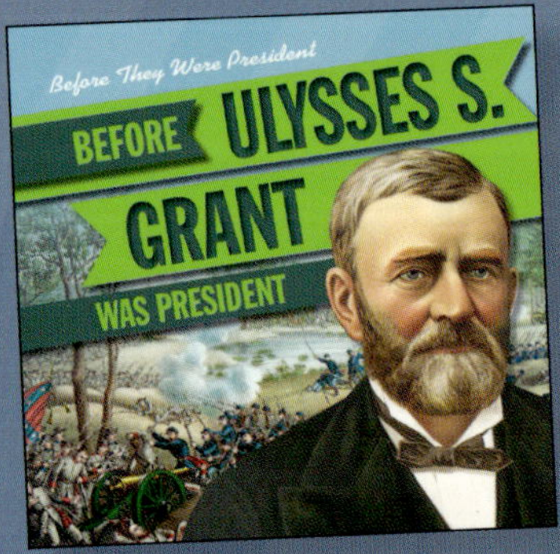

Levels: GR: M; DRA: 28

ISBN: 9781538232521
6-pack ISBN: 9781538232538
9 781538 232521

Gareth Stevens
PUBLISHING

NATIVE PEOPLES OF NORTH AMERICA

Native Peoples of THE GREAT PLAINS

Lynda Arnéz